BAXTER
Needs a Home

by Liam O'Donnell   Illustrated by Robert Hynes

Book Copyright © 2004 Trudy Corporation

Published by Soundprints Division of Trudy Corporation, Norwalk, Connecticut.

Book design: Marcin D. Pilchowski
Editor: Laura Gates Galvin
Editorial assistance: Brian E. Giblin

First Edition 2004
10 9 8 7 6 5 4 3 2 1
Printed in China

Acknowledgements:
    Soundprints would like to thank Joanne Clevenger and all the helpful staff and veterinarians at the American Veterinary Medical Association.

Library of Congress Cataloging-in-Publication Data

O'Donnell, Liam, 1970-
    Baxter needs a home / by Liam O'Donnell ; illustrated by Robert Hynes.--1st ed.
      p. cm. -- (Pet tales)
    Summary: Baxter, a tabby cat who has been abandoned by his former family, is rescued from the city streets by the owner of a bookstore.
    ISBN 1-59249-297-5 (large pbk.) -- ISBN 1-59249-298-3 (small pbk.)
      [1. Animal rescue--Fiction. 2. Cats--Fiction.] I. Hynes, Robert, ill. II. Title. III. Series.

    PZ7.O2397Bax 2004
    [E]--dc22
                                                                    2004002647

BAXTER
Needs a Home

by Liam O'Donnell   Illustrated by Robert Hynes

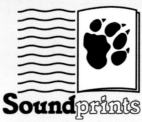

Soundprints

It is springtime and the city is wet with rain. People hurry along the crowded streets trying to stay dry. Nobody notices a thin tabby cat huddling under a trashcan. His name is Baxter and he doesn't have a home. Not long ago, Baxter lived in an apartment with a family. But his family moved away and left Baxter behind. Now he is wet, hungry and alone.

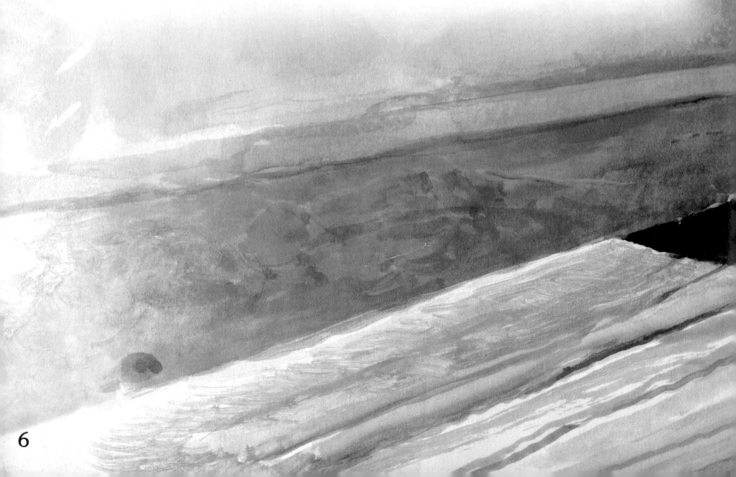

Baxter has seen other cats living on the streets. The nights are cold and food is hard to find. Cats can easily become sick without food, shelter and health care. Baxter's ear is very sore and it itches all the time. He needs to see a veterinarian soon.

Baxter has roamed the city looking for a new home but he has never been to this busy street. Will he find a family here? There are many people, but nobody seems to want Baxter.

Baxter comes to the entrance of a fruit seller's shop. It is brightly lit and is full of food. Baxter enters the small shop. The owner stacks oranges in a neat pile. Baxter rubs himself against the tall man's legs. "Go away," the fruit seller says. "I don't need a cat tripping my customers!"

Baxter races out of the fruit seller's shop. He passes a clothing store. It looks warm and dry. Baxter peers into the doorway. A lady sitting behind the sales desk smiles when she sees the hungry tabby.

Baxter takes a step into the store. Two large Siamese cats emerge from under a clothing rack and block Baxter's path. The Siamese cats hiss loudly at Baxter. This is their store and they do not want another cat here. Baxter wants a home, not a fight. He runs back into the rain.

Back on the street, Baxter feels lost and sleepy. The rain soaks through his fur. There is no room in this busy city for another cat. Baxter's ear aches and he is cold and wet. He starts walking toward the park across the street, hoping to find a dry place to take a nap.

47

BOOKS

Baxter carefully crosses the busy road and dashes into the park. The air is fresh with rain and the wet grass feels cool beneath his tired paws. The park is empty except for a family having a picnic under a gazebo. There is a father, a mother and a little girl, just like Baxter's old family. Baxter sprints to the little shelter.

He meows softly from the edge of the gazebo. The little girl smiles at him. She has kind eyes and gives Baxter some tuna from her sandwich. He snaps up the delicious fish in a single bite. He meows for more, but the family has finished their lunch. The little girl strokes Baxter's wet fur. She pats his furry head and runs back to her family. Baxter meows sadly and watches the family walk away.

Baxter races away from the gazebo and runs into the busy road. A bus rumbles along, heading straight for Baxter! The driver presses the brakes and honks the horn loudly. He is travelling too fast and cannot stop in time! Baxter is confused and doesn't know where to jump. Suddenly, a man reaches out from the curb and lifts Baxter out of the way of the bus.

Baxter struggles but the man's hands are strong. "You are safe, little friend." The man smiles through his bushy moustache. "My name is Hector." Hector carries Baxter into his bookstore. "My children are all gone and I am alone too." He pours some water into a bowl for Baxter. "Maybe you can live with me and we can keep each other company."

That night, Baxter sleeps on a warm blanket in Hector's apartment above the bookstore. The next morning they visit a veterinarian. In the waiting room, Baxter sits on Hector's lap and purrs quietly. The veterinarian examines Baxter, cleans and medicates his ears and gives him vaccinations to protect him against getting sick. The veterinarian also gives Baxter a collar with tags so he will never get lost again.

The spring rains turn into summer sunshine. Baxter's ear doesn't itch anymore and his belly is never empty. Hector takes good care of Baxter and Baxter takes good care of Hector and the busy bookstore. During the day, he perches proudly on a high shelf. From there, he meows loudly to the customers welcoming them all to his new home.

Pet Health and Safety Tips

• Stray animals should be taken to your veterinarian before you give them a home. Your veterinarian will perform a complete health checkup and will let you know whether it is safe to let the animal live in your house. Your veterinarian can also give you good advice on how to best care for your new pet.

• Your pet should always have clean water, nutritious food, and a warm and safe place to rest. Regular visits to your veterinarian are also important for your pet's good health.

• If your family can no longer care for your pet, don't put your pet out on the street like Baxter. Instead, ask your veterinarian for advice on finding your pet a new home.

• Because animals may wander away by accident, ensure that your pet is returned to you by making sure that everyone knows it is yours. Place a tag on its collar or, for identification that cannot be lost, have your veterinarian apply a tattoo or place a microchip (an electronic device that can be read by a special instrument) under your pet's skin.

GLOSSARY

Gazebo: An unenclosed, freestanding, roofed structure.

Tabby: A domestic cat with a striped and mottled coat.

Vaccination: Health products (usually injections) given to protect against disease.

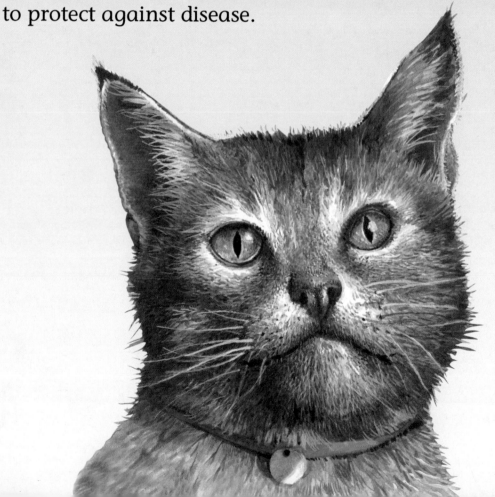

A Real-Life Pet Tale

Like Baxter, Tigger Too is one lucky cat. The stray cat found her way to the Gates' motor home while it was parked in a campground in the southern Utah desert. Chuck and Barbara Gates immediately adopted the cat and brought her to a veterinarian for medical treatment. Tigger is now healthy and loves to travel across the U.S. in the Gates' motor home. Tigger Too was named after the first cat the Gates family had for 19 years whose name was Tigger and who, coincidentally, looked exactly like Tigger Too!